Closed Out

ROSS PEARCE

Illustrated by David Dickson

sundance™
A Haights Cross Communications Company

The Characters

Kevin

Dad

Matthew

Grandmother

The Story Setting

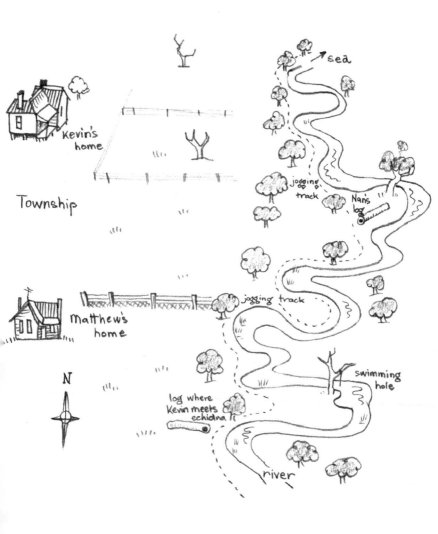

Kevin's home

Township

Matthew's home

sea

jogging track

Nan's log

jogging track

swimming hole

N

log where Kevin meets echidna

river

TABLE OF CONTENTS

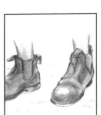

CHAPTER 1

A Silent Meeting

A leathery, black creature poked out from beneath the rotting log. Its thin, flickering tongue searched the air. The movement caught Kevin's eye. No, it couldn't be a snake. Maybe a lizard, he thought.

Curved claws scraped aside the leaves,
and a furry, funnel-shaped head
appeared. It was an echidna (i-kid-na).
It looked just like the one in the book
Kevin read before he and his dad moved
to Australia.

The echidna lumbered slowly forward. Its long black snout searched from side to side for anything edible. Suddenly it stopped, wary of danger.

Kevin could see the cream and black quills, like sharpened knitting needles, lying flat over its back. The boy and the echidna stood still, staring at each other.

Kevin could feel the warm afternoon sun on his back, but all of his other senses were focused on the echidna.

"You're a prickly little creature," Kevin said. "I wouldn't let you into my house. You're too prickly."

The echidna raised its snout and beady eyes toward Kevin. "You're not prickly, Kevin, so why aren't you allowed in? Why are you closed out?"

The thought was in Kevin's mind as if the echidna had spoken.

Kevin's shout shattered the quiet. "Get lost, echidna! You know nothing. I'm allowed into any place I want to go. Now get out of here."

For a second longer, the echidna looked at Kevin. Then it ambled off.

Kevin felt sad, but he quickly smothered that feeling with anger. Jumping up, he kicked at the log where he had first seen the echidna.

"Talking echidnas! What a joke!" he grumbled. "I'd better go and get dinner started." He headed home.

CHAPTER 2

Peeling Potatoes

Kevin opened the refrigerator and sighed. It was empty except for six cans of soda.

Kevin began peeling some potatoes. He wondered what Mom would have thought of the meals they'd been eating lately.

When Mom was alive, they'd had all kinds of feasts. His parents used to see who could make the most delicious dinners. His mother would make the greatest pasta dishes with fresh sauces.

Dad would work for hours on his Chinese and Thai dishes, making piles of finely sliced ingredients. Then, with arms flying, each pile was thrown into the smoking wok, making a mighty sizzle.

Dad didn't bother to cook much anymore.
He still cooked, but only ordinary—very
ordinary—food.

Kevin heard the screen door swing open,
and his father come in.

"Hi, Kevin. Survive the day OK?"

Kevin didn't answer. He stayed bent over the sink peeling potatoes.

Familiar sounds filled the room. Kevin heard the click of the fridge door and the hiss of a can opening. Then he heard the rustle of the newspaper.

"Thanks for getting the potatoes started. I bought some chicken," said Dad. "Let's get a pizza tomorrow night."

Kevin turned around to nod his head in agreement, but his father's head was already behind the newspaper.

CHAPTER 3

Dreaming

Kevin hadn't dreamed about the echidna, but he woke up thinking about it. He lay curled under the blanket, lost in thought, not ready to face a new day.

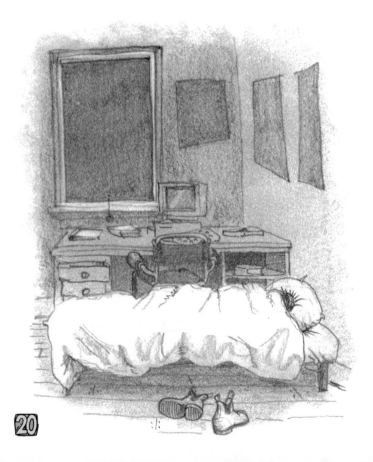

He could see the echidna so clearly—its black-tipped, creamy quills and the coarse, black hair of its face. Its shining eyes were a bright contrast to the dull blackness of its rubbery snout.

He could still hear the words, "You're not prickly, Kevin, so why aren't you allowed in? Why are you closed out?"

What does it mean? I'm allowed into any place, Kevin thought.

Yet somehow he knew that the echidna was right. He knew that he had to find out what it meant. But how? Who could possibly know what this spiny animal meant? He had to find the answer.

Maybe his friend Matthew would know. Matthew was an Aborigine, a native Australian. The Aborigines had lived here for thousands of years. They knew all about the country and its native creatures.

Kevin went to find Matthew after breakfast. "How long has your family lived here?" he asked Matthew.

"For over forty thousand years. That's something to be proud of," said Matthew.

"Do you know about native animals, like echidnas?" Kevin questioned further.

"No, Kev, I'm more into pizzas than porcupines. Are you going to the game?" said Matthew.

Kevin persisted. "But don't Aborigines know about nature and all that?"

"What's up, Kev? You sound like my grandmother, talking about all that traditional stuff."

"Can I talk to your grandmother about the traditional stuff?" Kevin asked.

"I guess so. She's given up on me. I'm more interested in sports," Matthew said.

Matthew was good at sports. He was good at schoolwork, too. And everyone liked Matthew. Kevin envied how everything seemed to be so easy for Matthew. It was so hard for him.

"Would you do that Matthew? Would you ask your grandmother to tell me about echidnas?" Kevin asked urgently.

"OK, OK. I'll ask my grandmother to talk to you. I'll ask her tonight and let you know tomorrow," Matthew said.

Kevin was excited, but a little scared. Now he would find out just what the meeting with the echidna was all about.

CHAPTER 4

Grandmother

Matthew introduced Kevin to his grandmother, and then he left them alone to talk. Sitting in the shade, they watched a large bird dry its outstretched wings on a branch above the river.

Kevin's urgency to learn all about the echidna was gone. He felt strangely at home with Matthew's grandmother.

Kevin felt like he could sit there forever, and Grandmother would ask nothing of him. But he needed to know what the echidna meant.

"Would you tell me about echidnas?"

"What would you like to tell me about echidnas, Kevin?"

"I think one spoke to me, but I don't know what it meant," said Kevin slowly.

"The echidna is my totem, so perhaps I can help you understand its meaning."

"What do you mean by totem?" asked Kevin.

"The full meaning of the totem is very complex, Kevin. Perhaps one day, if you want to know, I'll teach you some of our traditional ways. For now let's just say that we all have a totem."

"Our totem helps us understand how we belong to our family and tribe and to the world. It provides us with what we need. Perhaps the echidna is showing you what you need," said Grandmother.

Kevin exploded, "But I don't even know what it meant! The stupid thing told me something I can't understand."

Kevin froze. Had his anger ruined his chance to find out? He looked at the woman, but her soft eyes held no anger.

"Why would an echidna talk to me? I don't want anything to do with something that prickly. It's so prickly even its parents wouldn't want to hug it."

"Why did you tell the echidna it was too prickly to be let in?" Grandmother asked.

Somehow Kevin started telling her about how things had been before he and his dad moved to Australia, and how they were now. Grandmother watched and listened. Eventually Kevin ran out of words.

"Perhaps you should seek out the echidna again, Kevin. Ask and listen to your heart. Maybe you will understand the message this time."

Kevin smiled into the wise face. "When I figure this out, I'd like to learn more about totems and traditional things."

"There is much to learn. I'll gladly share some of our knowledge with you." She smiled warmly at him.

"Thanks for the talk. I'll let you know how things go," Kevin said.

Thinking It Through

Kevin walked home, puzzled about how Matthew's grandmother made him feel so confident. He didn't understand all of what she said. She seemed so wise, yet she hadn't said much at all. Maybe being smart was more about listening than talking.

His thoughts were interrupted by Matthew jogging toward him.

"I'm just going to walk my grandmother home. How did it go? Did you learn much about Australia?" Matthew asked.

"Your grandmother is great, Matthew.
She knows a lot of important stuff.
She's going to teach me some of your
traditional knowledge."

"Yeah? You think it's worth knowing?" Matthew called as he ran on.

"It must be worth knowing if it's survived over forty thousand years," Kevin shouted back.

Matthew jogged on, but he was surprised that this American boy was interested in his culture. It was so often ignored.

Matthew's grandmother was sitting right where he had left her. He felt a great warmth for her. He thought, maybe I should listen to my grandmother more carefully. It won't be good if Kevin knows more about my culture than I do.

CHAPTER 6

Kevin's Echidna

No matter how hard he tried, Kevin could not make the echidna come out from beneath the log. The sun was on Kevin's back, and the countryside hummed, but the echidna would not appear.

Kevin began to think about the Aboriginal woman and the feeling he had enjoyed as he sat and talked with her. Her words came back to him now.

"Ask, and listen to your heart."

How can I ask the echidna anything when it's not here to ask? Kevin thought. I have to figure this out. I really need to know what it means.

He remembered the echidna's words,
"Why are you closed out?"

"Of what? What do I feel closed out of?"
he whispered.

Suddenly, the answer came. I'm closed
out of my dad's life, Kevin realized.
I need Dad to let me back into his life.
I need him to love me and hug me like he
used to, especially now that Mom's gone.

Kevin was stunned by how simple the answer was. It was so obvious. His father had changed since his mother had died. They had never really talked about it. It was too painful. Kevin knew what he had to do.

CHAPTER 7

Jumping In

Kevin sat at the table, looking at his empty plate. He was trying to build up the courage to talk to his dad. It had to be done. It was the whole purpose of his meeting with the echidna.

Being afraid always reminded him of his first dive off the old tree back home.

"Come on, Kevin. You can do it. You've been practicing all summer!"

"Yeah, Kev! It'll be great! My dad taught me how to dive here."

Kevin had climbed lots of trees before, and he had dived into the pond from the bank. But he had never climbed a tree and dived off a branch. It was scary to be that high over the water.

He held his breath and plunged into the deep, cool water. It wasn't the greatest dive he had ever done, but as he surfaced, his fear was gone. He was filled with a great sense of satisfaction. His friends clapped. Kevin never forgot that experience, and now he said to himself, "That's the way to go. Just dive in."

"Dad, why have you shut me out of your life?" Kevin blurted out.

"What?" His father peered over the newspaper.

Kevin was again on the high branch. Would Dad make sense of this "closed out" business, or would he just laugh it off? Kevin wasn't sure.

Kevin answered quietly, "It's like you're living somewhere else, Dad. Since it's just been the two of us, you don't pay attention to me. I need you," Kevin said. "It's tough enough without Mom . . ."

His dad sat looking at him and then got up and went outside, the screen door banging behind him. Kevin stayed put. However Dad wanted to take it, Kevin knew inside that he had to say what he said. He thought of the echidna in the little clearing, staring at him.

Eventually he heard his father come back
into the house. Dad came into the kitchen
and propped himself against the sink.
He looked straight at Kevin.

"You're right, Kevin. I haven't been much of a father to you lately. I don't think I've been able to . . . I don't know, to reach out to anyone. But it's time I do."

"Yeah," was all Kevin could say. He saw his dad struggling with his pain.

"Why don't I cook up a great Chinese meal for us tomorrow? I'll leave work early and pick up everything we need on the way home. You can invite Matthew."

"That'd be great, Dad. I'll give you a hand with it. I'm sick of chicken and mashed potatoes."

"No more chicken for a while. And if I forget, you just remind me."

"OK, Dad. I will." Kevin grinned. His dad smiled back.

GLOSSARY

ambled
walked in a slow
and easy way

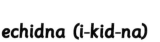

echidna (i-kid-na)
a spiky, ant-eating animal found
in Australia and New Guinea

lumbered
moved in a
clumsy way

quills

the spikes covering an echidna
or a porcupine

totem

an animal or plant
that serves as a
symbol of a family
or clan

wary
careful; on guard

Talking with the Author and the Illustrator

Ross Pearce (author)

What is your favorite smell?
  Dogs: big dogs, small dog, all sorts of dogs.
  They smell great—even when they have been
  playing in the rain.

What do you keep under your bed?
  Secret memories: my bird egg collection, a piece
  of coal I took from deep in a mine in Scotland,
  a photo of my pet bird, and other private things.

David Dickson (illustrator)

What is your favorite smell?
  Fresh parsley.

What day of the year do you like best?
  Any day I am fishing.

Published by Sundance Publishing
P.O. Box 1326, 234 Taylor Street, Littleton, MA 01460
800-343-8204
www.sundancepub.com

Copyright © text Ross Pearce
Copyright © illustrations David Dickson

First published 2000 as Sparklers by
Blake Education, Locked Bag 2022, Glebe 2037, Australia
Exclusive United States Distribution: Sundance Publishing

ISBN 0-7608-6976-6

sundance™
A Haights Cross Communications Company